NODDY

Here Comes Noddy

by Enid Blyton

The Five Mile Press

Everyone in Toyland knew little Noddy and his red-and-yellow car. They always waved to him when he drove down the streets with a passenger in his little taxi.

'Parp-parp!' went Noddy's horn as he hooted at three little dolls in the road. They scuttled out of the way quickly.

'There goes Noddy and his taxi! Look at his head nid-nodding as he drives. Did you hear the little bell jingling on his hat?'

Up and down Toyland went little Noddy in his car, taking people here, there and everywhere. Mr Tubby was always needing a lift somewhere. And when Noddy took Mary Mouse to catch the train one day he had to put her six children on the back of the car.

Once, Noddy took the skittles out to the country for a picnic. It was a very, very tight squeeze to get them all in the car beside him.

Another time he took a toy dog, who saw a toy cat in the street and jumped right out of the car to chase her. By the time Noddy had stopped the car and looked round they were nowhere to be seen. So he lost that passenger and didn't get any money.

'I shan't take dogs again,' said Noddy to himself. 'Hello, who's this wanting a taxi?'

It was one of the elephants out of Noah's Ark. He had got the day off for a holiday and he wanted to go into the wood and try to knock down trees.

'That's what real elephants do,' he told Noddy, trying to get into the car. 'I'm going to knock down trees, too, just to show everyone I'm as good as a real elephant.'

Noddy was alarmed. 'You don't need to knock down trees for that,' he said. 'That's silly and dangerous.'

The elephant tried to climb into the car, but Noddy pushed him out. 'Let me in,' said the elephant. 'I might even lift up your car in my trunk and drop it down hard.'

'You're a very bad elephant,' said Noddy fiercely.

The elephant pushed little Noddy hard till he was all squashed up in his driving seat. Then he sat down so suddenly that the door of the car burst open. It wouldn't shut.

'Please get out,' begged little Noddy. 'You will break my car. I'm not going to let you knock down trees.'

But the elephant wouldn't get out.

'This is wonderful,' said the elephant, enjoying himself. 'I've never been in a car before. Oh, how nice it is – *bumpity-bumpity-bumpity-bump!* Can I sound the hooter?'

'No, you can't,' said Noddy.

But the elephant did, of course, and everybody jumped as Noddy's car went along hooting loudly. Then the elephant settled down to have a nap. Noddy watched until the elephant's eyes closed and a little snore came out of his mouth. Then Noddy returned to Toyland. He drove right up to the big Noah's Ark. Mr Noah was there, and Noddy beckoned to him.

'This elephant tried to make me take him to the woods to knock down trees. Please will you tell him off, Mr Noah?'

'Certainly!' said Mr Noah, and he tapped the big elephant smartly on the trunk. The toy animal opened his eyes with a jump.

'Out you get, elephant,' said Mr Noah sternly. 'Go into the ark, put yourself in a corner – and WAIT FOR ME!'

The elephant hung his head and lumbered into the ark.

'Thanks, Mr Noah,' said Noddy, turning the car around again. 'Let me know when you and Mrs Noah want a ride. I'll take you in my car!' And off he went, very pleased to have got rid of the big, bad elephant!

THE ELEPHANT INSISTED ON RIDING IN NODDY'S
CAR BUT WHEN HE SQUEEZED HIMSELF IN,
THE DOOR BURST OPEN AND WOULDN'T SHUT.

Noddy was always pleased when his day's work was done and he could drive home to his little house. He had a dear little home, which he and his friend Big-Ears had made together, out of toy bricks. It was called House-for-One because it was so small.

It didn't have a garage at first. When Noddy had saved a little money he went and got some more toy bricks in a box.

Then he took them out and built the tiny garage at the side of House-for-One. The little red-and-yellow car sleeps there at night, as cosy as can be.

In the morning, Noddy wakes up, takes off his little pyjamas and has a bath in a tub he bought for himself, because he hasn't got a bathroom. When he is dressed, he puts on his cap with the tinkling bell.

He always sings when he brushes his mop of hair and cleans his shoes.

'I've cleaned my teeth
And I've brushed my hair,
I've polished my shoes
And I've time to spare
To drink my milk
And to eat my bread,
And I've plenty of time
To nod my head.
Nid-diddy-nod,
Nid-diddy-nod!'

It's a funny little song, and Mr and Mrs Tubby, the bears who live next door, like to hear it every morning.

One morning there was a knock at Noddy's little front door. 'Hey, Noddy! Are you there? Get out your car and take me to the Village of Bouncing Balls, will you?'

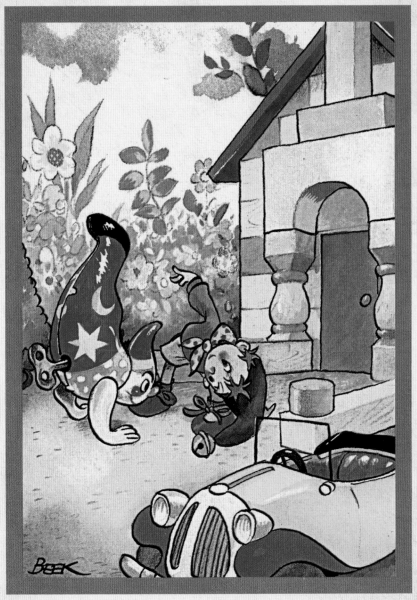

THE CLOCKWORK CLOWN ASKED IF NODDY COULD
TAKE HIM TO THE VILLAGE OF THE BOUNCING BALLS.

Noddy opened the door. The clockwork clown was outside in the garden. He was going head-over-heels all over the place. That was the way he usually went along.

'Do stop, Clown,' said Noddy. 'You always make me feel so dizzy. Whatever do you want to go to the Village of Bouncing Balls for?'

'I want to get a little one for myself,' said the clown, standing up for a moment. 'I plan to do a good trick with it – walk on it all around the circus ring when I perform.'

'I should hate to try to walk on a ball,' said Noddy. 'Oh, don't start going head-over-heels again. Look, you've squashed one of my plants.'

The clown stood up again. 'Are you ready?' he said. 'Well, get your car out then. I'm in a hurry.'

Noddy got his car out and the clown got in.

'Now listen,' said Noddy. 'If you begin going head-over-heels in and out of the car, I'll leave you behind! You'd give me such a fright that I would run into a lamp post or something.'

'All right,' said the clown. 'Though I would rather like to see you knock a lamp post down. BANG! What a noise it would make.'

'Now you're being silly,' said Noddy, and away they went. The clown began to sing at the top of his voice.

'If I were a bouncing ball
I'd bounce myself so high
That I'd knock all the clouds away
And make a hole in the sky.'

Noddy began to laugh. 'Now don't you teach silly ideas to the bouncing balls,' he said. 'They're quite mad enough already.'

'Here we are,' said the clown, as he saw the balls bouncing in the distance. 'We didn't take long to get here. Wait for me, Noddy, and I'll go and get a really nice little ball.'

The clown went off, head-over-heels, as fast as ever he could. A ball bounced up and then bounced itself all round the car.

'Don't,' said Noddy. 'If you make a mistake and bounce on my car you'll squash it flat. And me, too.'

Another ball came up and bounced round. Noddy didn't like it at all. He thought he would drive off and run his car down a little rabbit burrow. Then he would be safe.

But the balls bounced after him, and Noddy was so scared that he couldn't see where he was going. He ran straight into two little balls standing together in the road talking.

'Whoooooooooo!' said one of the balls, and Noddy gazed in dismay at a big dent he had made in the rubber ball. There was a hole there, too, and the 'whooooo' noise was the air coming out.

'Oh, sorry,' said Noddy – but in a trice all kinds of balls came bouncing up and surrounded the little car.

The clockwork clown came hurrying up, too, with a little ball bouncing beside him. 'Now what have you done, Noddy?' he said. 'Dented a ball? How careless of you! My word – how angry these balls look. Come on – we'd better go.'

So off they went at top speed – but it was a horrid drive because all the balls did their best to bounce on top of the car. Noddy drove to and fro and zigzagged all the way, trying to get out of the way of the angry balls.

One knocked the clown's hat off, and one made a car lamp crooked. When they left Bouncing Ball Village there was only one ball bouncing merrily after the car.

'You needn't mind that one,' said the clown. 'It's mine – to perform that trick on, you know. It will follow us like a dog.'

And so it did. *Bouncity-bouncity-bounce*, it went, and though Noddy was afraid it might bump into the car, it didn't.

The little nodding man was very, very glad when he got back to his own town again. 'I shall never take anyone to the Village of Bouncing Balls again,' he said. 'It's too dangerous. You'll have to pay me double fare, Clown, for my trouble.'

> 'Double, double,
> For your trouble,
> I'm quite willing,
> Here's a shilling,'

'A shilling,' said the clown, and handed over a nice round silver shilling. He got out and called to his little ball. It rolled up to him like a good, obedient little dog!

'No more bouncing, please,' said the clown. 'I want to practise walking on you. Now keep still and I'll jump up on you.'

And away down the street the two of them went, the clown walking cleverly on the ball as it rolled along.

'I do hope it won't begin to bounce when the clown is walking on it,' said Noddy to himself. 'He would get a shock! Now I'll go and get some dinner. I really feel hungry after that peculiar visit to the Village of Bouncing Balls.'

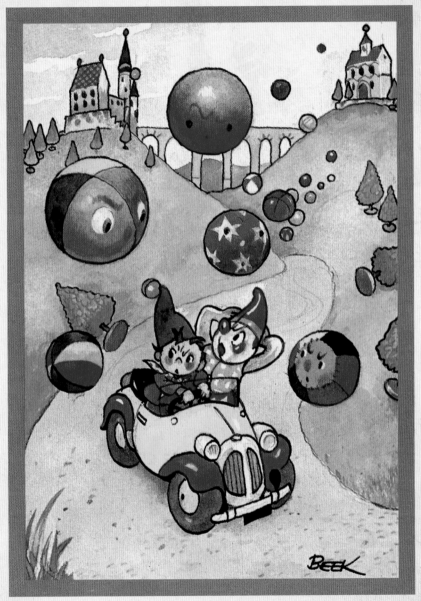

THE ANGRY BOUNCING BALLS CHASED NODDY AND
THE CLOCKWORK CLOWN RIGHT OUT OF TOWN.

One day Noddy got a message from Mr Straw, the farmer at the toy farm.

'Please will you come and fetch some of my hens and ducks and take them to market for me? My horse has hurt his leg and he can't take the farm cart to market.'

'Well, it will be a change to take hens and ducks in my car instead of toys,' said Noddy to himself. 'I hope they'll be good.'

When he got to the farm, he hooted outside the farmhouse door.

Mrs Straw, the farmer's wife, came to the door, smiling. 'Oh, hello, little Noddy,' she said. 'Can you drive your car over the fields to the hen-house there? Mr Straw has the hens and ducks ready.'

Noddy drove carefully over the fields. He had to open a gate once and drive through it. And, oh dear me, there was a goat there who didn't like Noddy coming into his field at all.

He ran at the car and butted it hard. Up into the air it went, with Noddy in it, and right over the hedge!

Noddy fell out into the hedge, and the car fell splash into a pond. The ducks fled off the water, quacking in fear.

The farmer stared in surprise at Noddy. 'Do you usually try to drive your car over hedges?' he said.

'It was your goat,' said Noddy crossly. 'Come and get me down, Mr Straw. I'm stuck up in this hedge. It's a very good thing that my body is wooden, or these prickles would be hurting me!'

Mr Straw got him down. They went and looked at the car. It was upside down in the water. Noddy felt very miserable indeed.

He and the farmer tried to get it out, but they couldn't.

'You'll have to empty the pond,' said Noddy. 'I can't lose my car.'

So Mr Straw called to all his cows and donkeys and sheep and pigs. 'Buttercup, Daisy, Woolly, Long-Ears, come here, all of you!'

They all came, about twelve of them, and stood looking at the car in the pond.

MR STRAW CALLED TO THE ANIMALS TO DRINK FROM THE
POND SO THAT NODDY COULD RETRIEVE HIS CAR.

'Drink,' said Mr Straw. 'Drink as much as you can. Quickly, now!'

So Buttercup, Daisy, Woolly, Long-Ears and all the rest of the toy farm animals bent their heads and drank.

The water sank lower and lower – and at last the pond was almost empty. 'Your animals look very fat now,' said Noddy, rather alarmed. 'Tell them to stop. We can get the car now.'

So the animals stopped drinking, and Mr Straw and Noddy tugged the little car the right way up, and then wheeled it to the bank, through the mud. Noddy was very dirty when he had finished, and so was Mr Straw.

'I must go home and have a bath,' said Noddy. 'And I must wash my car, too. Oh dear – what a dreadful morning. I'll be back for your hens and ducks this afternoon, Mr Straw.'

Well, he went back that afternoon, quite clean, but as his clothes weren't dry, Mrs Tubby, the teddy bear next door, had lent him a pair of Mr Tubby's old blue trousers, which were much too big for him, and a little coat of her own. He really looked very peculiar.

'Just leave the hens with my brother at the market,' said Mr Straw. 'Here's sixpence for their fare. And if they lay any eggs on the way you can have them, to make up for my goat butting you.'

The hens and ducks squashed together on the seat beside Noddy. They were excited about their ride, and quacked and clucked loudly.

'Now hold tightly,' said Noddy. 'And nobody is to fly off.'

And off they went. One of the hens was frightened and crept onto Noddy's knee, which made it difficult for him to drive the car. He got to market, found Mr Straw's brother, and gave him all the excited birds.

Will you believe it – when Noddy got back into the car to drive home, there were eleven eggs on the seat beside him! Eleven! Noddy stared at them in delight.

'Eleven eggs for my breakfast!' he said. 'No, ten, because I must give Mrs Tubby one for lending me these clothes. What luck!'

Noddy was really a very busy little taxi driver indeed. His car was used a dozen times a day for this and that.

He was so friendly and polite that everyone liked him. He gave the tiny dolls rides for nothing. He always picked up the little clockwork mouse when he saw him hurrying to catch the toy train. And if he met a pixie or a brownie he stopped to give them a lift.

And then one day a goblin called on him. 'Are you Noddy, the little nodding man, who has a car?' asked the goblin, putting his head round the door and making Noddy jump.

'Yes. But please don't peep round like that. There's a knocker on the door,' said Noddy. 'What do you want?'

'I want to go to a party in the Dark Wood at midnight,' said the goblin.

'Oh – I don't think I want to go to the Dark Wood in the middle of the night,' said Noddy. 'It's rather frightening there.'

'I'll give you a bag of sixpences if you'll take me,' said the goblin, and he jingled the money in his pocket. He looked round Noddy's little house. 'They would buy you a new carpet, and a new armchair and a much nicer clock.'

A bag of sixpences! Dear, dear – that sounded a lot of money. Noddy thought about it, nodding his head until the bell on his hat jingled a tune.

'All right,' he said at last, 'I'll take you. But I don't like it much. I've done hardly any driving at night, and my lamps aren't very good. And I really don't like the Dark Wood, even in the daytime.'

'Pooh,' said the goblin. 'I'll be with you, won't I? You can come to the party, too, if you like, and take me back home. That will be two bags of sixpences then.'

Noddy nodded his head madly. Two bags of sixpences! Why, he would be very, very rich – and all for a drive in the middle of the night to the Dark Wood. Who cared about the Dark Wood? Anyway, the moon would be shining.

At twelve o'clock that night Noddy got out his little car. He jumped when a voice came out of the darkness. 'Are you ready? I'm here!'

It was the goblin. It was so dark that Noddy couldn't see him at all. Then Noddy took a step forwards and bumped straight into him.

'Oh, sorry,' he said. 'Yes, I'm ready. Here is the car. Jump in.'

The goblin climbed in. Noddy switched on the lights of the little car. They weren't very good, only just enough to see by as he went down the streets of Toy Town. The goblin began to sing a peculiar song.

> *'It isn't very good*
> *In the Dark Dark Wood*
> *In the middle of the night*
> *When there isn't any light;*
> *It isn't very good*
> *In the Dark Dark Wood.'*

'Don't sing that,' said Noddy. 'You make me nervous. I shall drive into a tree or something. Be quiet, Goblin.'

So the goblin was quiet, but he kept making little chuckling noises, which Noddy didn't like at all.

'I wish I hadn't come,' Noddy thought. 'I do wish I hadn't come!'

'I'LL GIVE YOU A BAG OF SIXPENCES IF YOU TAKE ME TO
A PARTY IN THE DARK WOODS,' SAID THE GOBLIN.

Eventually they came to the Dark Wood. Although the moon was shining in the sky, the wood was just like its name – very, very dark. The lights on Noddy's little car made little bright paths between the trees.

'Where's this party of yours?' asked Noddy. 'I don't want to drive any deeper into the wood.'

'Well, stop just here, then,' said the goblin, and Noddy stopped. Where was the party? And the band? Where were the lights, and happy voices?

'It's so quiet,' he said to the goblin. 'Where is the party?'

'There isn't a party,' said the goblin in a very nasty sort of voice. 'This is a trap, Noddy. We want your car for ourselves. Get out at once!'

Noddy couldn't move an inch. He was so full of alarm that he couldn't say a word. A trap! Whose trap! And why did they want his car?

Then things happened very quickly. Three ugly faces suddenly appeared in the light of the car's lamps, and three goblins came running to the car. In a trice they had hold of poor Noddy and pulled him right out of his little car.

The goblin who had come with him took the wheel, laughing loudly. 'What did I tell you?' he said. 'It isn't very good in the Dark Dark Wood! Hey, you others, there's room for one beside me and two sitting on the back of the car.'

'Wait a minute,' said one of the other goblins. 'This little driver has got some rather nice clothes on. We might as well have those, too!'

'Oooh yes,' said another goblin. 'I'll have his lovely hat – it's got a jingle-bell at the top.'

'And I'll have his shirt and tie,' said a third goblin. He pulled them off poor little Noddy.

Then the driver leaned out and told the others to get him Noddy's dear little trousers and shoes.

Soon Noddy had no clothes on at all. He wriggled and shouted and wailed. 'No, no, no! I want my hat, I want my shirt. You bad, wicked goblin! How dare you steal my things!'

But it wasn't a bit of good. What could the little nodding man do against four wicked goblins? Nothing at all.

The goblins piled into the little red-and-yellow car. Two were in front, two sat in the back of the car. One of them had Noddy's hat on. The moon shone down on it suddenly through the trees and Noddy wailed loudly.

'My dear little hat! Oh, do, do leave me that!'

'Ha, ha, ho, ho!' laughed the bad goblins and drove off at top speed. 'R–r–r–r–r!' went the little car, and the sound grew fainter and fainter, till at last it couldn't be heard any more.

Noddy was all alone in the Dark Wood. He remembered the song of the goblin. 'It isn't very good in the Dark Dark Wood,' and he stood up, trembling.

'Help!' he called. 'Oh, help, help, HELP! I'm little Noddy and I'm all alone and LOST!'

Nobody answered Noddy. He stumbled along through the trees, tears running down his cheeks.

'I've lost my hat,
I've lost my car;
I simply don't know
Where they are!
I'm all alone;
Won't ANYBODY
Come to help
Poor little Noddy?'

He went on and on until he met a scared little mouse hurrying back to his hole. 'Mouse, mouse – tell me where I am!' called Noddy. 'Does anyone live near here?'

'There's only M-m-m-mister B-b-b-big-Ears,' said the mouse, frightened. 'Over there, see that toadstool house in the moonlight?'

Noddy gave a sudden squeal of joy that scared the mouse so much he fled down a rabbit hole in mistake for his own hole. Noddy's head began to nod again. Oh, Big-Ears, Big-Ears, are you really near?

He came to the little toadstool house where Big-Ears lived, and his head nodded in joy. He banged at the front door in the stalk, yelling, 'Big-Ears, Big-Ears, come and let me in!'

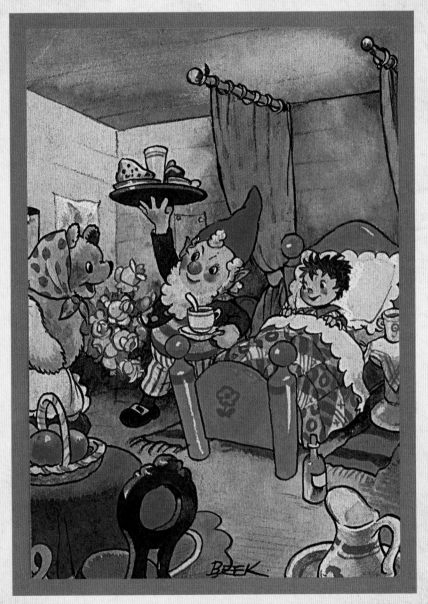

THE FOLK FROM TOY TOWN VISITED NODDY ALL DAY LONG,
BRINGING HIM GIFTS AND WARM WISHES TO GET BETTER.

Big-Ears the brownie put his head out of the window and stared in surprise and alarm at the little nodding man outside.

'Noddy! Is it you? What are you doing here in the middle of the night without your clothes? Are you mad, or am I dreaming?'

'Let me in,' shouted Noddy. 'I'm cold without any clothes!'

So Big-Ears let him in and was soon hearing Noddy's sad story. 'Even my dear little hat with a bell,' said Noddy with a sneeze.

'What a sneeze!' said Big-Ears, startled. 'Look, I'll lend you a coat and we'll hurry back to Toy Town and get Mr Plod the policeman. Then you must go straight to bed, or you'll catch a dreadful chill.'

They hurried to Toy Town and woke up Mr Plod, and he was most astonished to hear their tale. Then Big-Ears hurried Noddy back to the House-for-One, and put Noddy to bed with two hot water bottles. 'Now you can stay there, little Noddy,' he said. 'I'll soon put things right for you.'

Noddy fell asleep and Big-Ears thought about what to do. In the morning, Noddy awoke to find Big-Ears bringing him his breakfast.

'Now you stay in bed today,' said Big-Ears kindly. 'Don't worry about anything. I've had a very good idea.'

The news soon got around Toy Town that Noddy had been robbed. There were knocks on the door all day long!

'Can I come in?' called Mrs Tubby. 'I've brought you roses!'

'Can I come in?' cried someone else. 'I've brought you an ice-cream!' And in came Angela Golden-Hair, the pretty doll.

Rat-a-tat! In came the toy cat with a jigsaw puzzle to do. *Rat-a-tat!* That was the clockwork clown with two bananas and a peach. *Rat-a-tat-TAT!* That was Mr Straw with six brown eggs.

'Oh, thank you, thank you, thank you,' Noddy kept saying, and his head nodded happily. 'I am having a lovely time!'

When everyone had gone, Noddy called to Big-Ears. 'Tell me your very, very good idea, Big-Ears, please.'

Big-Ears proudly showed him a big notice. This was what he had printed on it:

WILL ANYONE WHO HEARS A BELL JINGLING PLEASE TELL BIG-EARS?

'Ooh – you mean the bell on my hat?' said Noddy. 'You think a goblin is wearing it – and its jingle will give away their hiding place? Oooh, what a very, very good idea!'

Well it really was, because not half an hour after Big-Ears had put up the notice outside the little nodding man's house, two small clockwork mice came shyly in.

'Please, Mr Big-Ears,' said one, 'we've heard a bell jingling.'

'Yes – we heard it inside the old hollow tree at the edge of the Dark Wood,' whispered the other little mouse. 'Not far from the stream, Mr Big-Ears.'

'Thank you,' said Big-Ears, delighted. 'That is just what I wanted to know. Here's a bit of cheese for both of you.'

The clockwork mice ran off. Big-Ears smiled at Noddy. 'Now we know where those wicked goblins are hiding – in that old hollow tree. Come to think of it, there's a hole at the bottom of the tree where they could hide the car. I'll tell Mr Plod the policeman at once!'

Off he went, and Noddy was so excited that his head nodded twice as fast as he lay in bed waiting for the next bit of news.

Mr Plod said he would only want a big toy dog, a very large sack, himself and Big-Ears. So they set off with Bongo, the largest toy dog in Toy Town, and a big sack over the policeman's shoulder.

'Ssh!' said Big-Ears, when they came near the hollow tree. 'Just send Bongo to bark at the bottom hole. Climb up to the other hole, and I'll come with you. Bongo will bark and frighten the goblins, and they will all climb quickly out of the top hole into our sack!'

Bongo ran to the hole at the bottom of the tree and barked loudly. 'Wuff, wuff, wuffy WUFF! WOOF, WOOF, WOOF!'

There were squeals and howls and wails and a scrabbling noise as the four goblins scrambled up to the top hole. Big-Ears was there, holding up the sack with Mr Plod.

'Tie them up,' said Mr Plod, and he and Big-Ears tied up the neck of the sack very tightly indeed.

'Now I'll get Noddy's little car,' said Big-Ears. He scrambled the hole and there was Noddy's tiny car! Big-Ears wheeled it out.

'If you'd like to put the sack of goblins in the car you can drive them off to the police station,' said Big-Ears. 'I'll go and get my bicycle and follow you. There wouldn't be room for me. My house is just nearby.'

So the policeman drove off with the sack of squealing goblins, and Big-Ears followed on his little bicycle, ringing the bell loudly.

They stopped outside House-for-One. Mr Plod hooted the horn. Parp-parp! Big-Ears rang his bell – *ring-ring-ring-ring!*

Noddy jumped out of bed and came to the window.

'Hello, there!' shouted Big-Ears. 'We've got a sack of goblins, and your car – and you'll soon have all your clothes back, too, once we've popped the goblins into prison!'

Noddy's head almost nodded itself off in joy. 'Hurry back with my clothes,' he cried, 'especially my little hat – and bring back a big, big cake, Big-Ears. We'll have a party because you've been so very, very clever!'

And so they did. Big-Ears came back and gave Noddy all his clothes again. He drove the little car safely back into its garage, and then they both had a big slice of cake.